Kitsune-Tsuki

Laura VanArendonk Baugh

Æclipse Press
Indianapolis, IN

To all those who asked me to

dedicate a book to them—

here it is.

But mostly, to my family and the Author.

Glossary

ashigaru — foot soldier

bakemono — any of several supernatural shapeshifting entities

bakeneko — cat spirit

biwa — a stringed instrument

daimyou — feudal lord

de gozaimasu, de gozaimashita — formal phrasing

-dono — formal honorific (now archaic)

doumo arigatou gozaimasu — thank you very much

futagokyoudai — twin brothers

Genji & Kaworu — Genji Hikaru and his son Kaworu, famed philanderers of Lady Murasaki's fictional *Genji Monogatari*

hakama — pleated leg garment

haori — men's jacket-type garment

hime — princess or daughter of a high house

hoshi no tama — "star-stone," a jewel or ball belonging to a *kitsune* inu — dog

inuoumono — dog hunt

kai — a syllable of mystical release

kanji — written characters imported from China

kata — choreographed movement or form

kekkai — mystic barrier

kimono — literally "clothing," but usually referring to the long body robe

kitsune — fox spirit

kitsune-mochi — fox possessor, a human who bound or used *kitsune*

kitsune-tsuki — state of being possessed by a fox spirit

koku — unit of measure, enough rice to feed one person for one year

konbanwa — good evening

kuji-in — "the nine syllables"

-kun — honorific to address one of lower status or, often, a young male

-me — a disparaging form of address

mononoke — general term for supernatural entity, usually harmful mudra — gesture or movement performed as part of spiritual ritual

oni — supernatural creature often compared to the Western ogre

onmyoudou — system of knowledge and mysticism which includes aspects of yin-yang, feng shui, astronomy, astrology, natural sciences, divination, calendar-keeping, etc. At one point a valued and vital government occupation with high position.

onmyouji — one who practices *onmyoudou*

ookami — wolf

origami — art of paper folding

sake — rice wine

-sama — more respectful honorific

samurai — warrior caste

-san — respectful honorific

shikigami — spirit assisting an *onmyouji*, often seen with folded paper or similar constructs

shouji — door or room-dividing screen. Today, *shouji* are generally of lattice and rice paper, but at this time, *shouji* were wood overlaid with paper like what is today called *fusuma*.

tatami — woven mat

tono — lord, honorific

torii — gate at shrine

wakizashi — short sword

youkai — any of many supernatural entities

Chapter 1

Tsurugu no Kiyomori bowed low over the polished floor. "I am at your service, *tono*."

"I am glad to hear it," answered Naka no Yoritomo. "We can be only relieved by the presence of an accomplished *onmyouji*. Your service in protecting our household and our new wife will be greatly appreciated and greatly rewarded."

"The thanks of the *daimyou* is recompense enough," replied Tsurugu. "I am grateful that you have honored one such as myself with this trust."

"You have been entrusted with more than this," Naka no Yoritomo said significantly. "You will find in your room an additional token of our faith."

Tsurugu bowed a final time and then followed a silent servant to his new room, observing the carefully-kept grounds with a casual eye. Naka no Yoritomo was a wealthy man and inclined to display it, in everything from his immaculate gardens to his hiring of an *onmyouji* mystic to protect his bride. Tsurugu's stay would be pleasant, provided he pleased the *daimyou*.

Naka no Yoritomo believed that a local *kitsune* meant to work mischief upon him or his new wife, Fujitani no Kaede. There had been strange incidents in the countryside of late, with objects of value disappearing and irrational stories offered by confused laborers for missing goods and missing hours. There had even been a recent case of *kitsune-tsuki* in the farmers' village below, a poor young girl possessed by a fox spirit and driven to madness. The villagers had beaten and burned her in an attempt to drive out the fox, but she had broken free and run screaming into the woods.

Privately, Tsurugu suspected the girl was simply mad, for bad blood or other causes, and not a victim of a fox at all. But it was little use to argue with the *daimyou*.

The servant paused to slide aside a *shouji* door. Before Tsurugu could enter, two figures came about the corner, moving side by side on the exterior walkway. He paused to regard them — two young men, perhaps sixteen, if the ages of servants mattered. They did not quite bow their heads deferentially, so he could clearly see their faces. They were handsome young men, and absolutely alike. Even had they averted their gaze fully, one would have guessed they were twins.

He entered his room. "Who are they?" he asked the servant who waited by his door.

"*Futagokyoudai*," he answered, "in the household of Kaede-dono." His tone betrayed his disapproval; a woman, even a widow, had no business bringing male servants, and certainly not such as those.

Tsurugu suppressed a smile. The women would be chattering about the twins, certainly, and a few of the men, no doubt. They were well-formed enough to forgive their lapse in etiquette; they would of course be kept matched together in service.

The servant left, and Tsurugu began to explore his new room. It was comfortably furnished, with thick *tatami* suitable for the *daimyou* himself, but he found no lacquered box or inked message from the lord as promised. Perhaps it would come later, he mused, and he occupied himself by opening his writing set and grinding ink as he looked out upon the groomed courtyard, darkening with evening. He selected a sheet and began to paint, concentrating on the more delicate brushstrokes he had never mastered. A tree branch came slowly into being on his page, mostly bare but with narrow buds promising spring beauty. He should compose a poem on his arrival here, something honoring Naka no Yoritomo and —

"*Konbanwa*," came a voice behind him. *Good evening*.

Tsurugu spun, spattering ink across his fresh paper. A man crouched comfortably in a corner of his room, dressed all in soft grey.

Tsurugu took a breath and composed himself. "You are sent from the *daimyou*."

"I am."

"You are one of his shadows."

A half-smile crooked the stranger's face. "A good way of saying it. I am the unseen eye, the unseen hand."

"You were certainly unseen." Tsurugu gestured. "Come and sit with me." He bowed slightly. "Tsurugu no Kiyomori *de gozaimasu*," he introduced himself.

"Kagemura no Shishio Hitoshi *de gozaimasu*," replied the man in grey, bowing in return. He hesitated. "I have been commanded to serve my lord in alliance with you, and in confidence. You have won his trust, or you would not have my name and face so readily."

Tsurugu took a small, unspoiled sheet of orange paper from his writing set and began to toy with it. "I am honored to meet you, Ookami-kun."

Shishio raised an eyebrow. "*Ookami?*" *Wolf?*

"Forgive me; I have an irrepressible habit of giving names to my fellows. In your case, however, it seems appropriate, as you would not be comfortable with my casual use of your own name. You are all in grey, a shadow among shadows — and whom should a fox fear more than a wolf?"

Shishio grinned. "Whom, indeed?" He settled comfortably across from Tsurugu. "Then I thank you for the gift of my new name."

"It is my pleasure." Tsurugu bowed his head and continued to fold the paper.

"What is your opinion, onmyouji-san? Why would a *kitsune* target my lord?" asked Shishio. "Is it a male, envious of his new wife's beauty? Or is it a young female, jealous of my lady's happiness?"

Tsurugu smiled. "Perhaps she is in love with the *daimyou* and wishes to marry him herself."

"My lord, in thrall to a fox woman?" Shishio recoiled in distaste. "It cannot be. We cannot allow it." He looked piercingly at

Tsurugu. "I hope we will not allow it. You will forgive me, I hope, onmyouji-san, if I ask your part in this. How will you serve my lord? Because if I find you are a common trickster who has for money claimed —"

"Please, Ookami-kun," interrupted Tsurugu mildly. He opened his hands to reveal an orange animal, a dog or wolf or fox. "A trickster I may be, but never common." He set the *origami* figure on the mat beside his knee and watched as it bounded toward Shishio.

Shishio twitched backward, his hands falling naturally to his weapon, and then caught himself as the paper figure cavorted harmlessly. "What is this?"

Tsurugu lowered his hand so that the little canid could jump into it. "Surely you have seen an *onmyouji*'s servants," he answered easily, "if you have seen a true *onmyouji*." He shifted his eyes from paper to Shishio.

"A *shikigami*?" Shishio blinked and then bowed. "I apologize for my insulting words," he offered. "I have seen only tricksters and diviners who took coin for word games. But it is clear my lord chose wisely when he asked you to help us."

Tsurugu smiled and whispered a word of release, letting the *shikigami* dispel and the orange paper lie still. "I hope we shall be good friends, Ookami-kun."

Shishio gave him a pleased look. "I hope so as well."

Chapter 2

The village girl had been found, bruised and burnt from her failed exorcism, and brought to her home again. She was weak with exposure and hunger, and she said little; it was hoped that the fox had left her while she hid and that she would recover as herself.

In the *daimyou*'s household, however, worry did not cease. If the fox had left the troubled girl, where had it gone? Or if it had not, what havoc would it wreak in the village?

Still, life must continue. Soldiers trained outside the house, farmers labored in the rice fields, women sewed *kimono* and *haori*. Shishio came in the evenings to discuss what he had heard of strange activity in the area. "Several *koku* of rice disappeared beside the Inari Shrine."

Tsurugu gave him a curious look. "Is that not more likely the work of common thieves than a *kitsune*?"

"Inari would not permit rice, the essence of her power and protection, to be stolen at her very shrine."

"Inari would not permit foxes to work mischief at her very shrine, either," he protested reasonably. White foxes were the goddess's symbol and guardians; a *kitsune* would respect the shrine. "I think a few of your shadows, set to secretly watch unguarded rice, might discover a thief much more mundane."

Shishio nodded slowly. "We will see. But what if it is the *kitsune*? I have heard that fox magic can make men see what is not. I would not have men killing one another because they see foxes instead of their comrades. I of course could —"

Tsurugu raised a hand. "I will come with you. I will set myself with you and, should we be enveloped in fox magic, I will dispel the illusion." He grinned. "That is presumably why the lord desired both an *onmyouji* and his *ookami*."

Shishio chuckled. "Then I will arrange for a tempting cargo of rice to draw out these bandits. But not immediately; it must not appear a response to this theft. It will merely be the next merchant to stop near the shrine."

"Of course."

Shishio tipped his head to one side, considering. "Could you not send a *shikigami* to watch the shrine?"

"From here? So far?" Tsurugu chuckled. "Abe no Seimei might do such a thing, but not I."

"Abe no Seimei...?"

"The greatest *onmyouji* ever to live. He might have sent one of the Twelve Heavenly Generals to confound and seize the thieves. But not I." He held up a finger. "It is said his mother was *kitsune*; that is what gave him much of his power."

"And yours was not?"

Tsurugu smiled. "Had I the blending of fox magic and human strength, I might have been a great *onmyouji* myself. But I am afraid I am merely Tsurugu no Kiyomori."

"Then I suppose you will have to do." Shishio glanced toward the door, lit from without by moonlight. "Yoritomo-dono will host a moon-gazing party soon," he said. "You will be invited, of course, and I will also be there." He smiled slyly; he would be less visible. "There will be a great number of guests; it would be an ideal time for a *kitsune* to assume a human shape and gain entrance."

"We will be watchful," Tsurugu assured him. He rose from the low table, feeling his legs stretch. "I would like to go out for a moment now, in fact. I have sat too long."

"I will come with you."

The elegant courtyard lay quiet in the night, lit by lanterns which already did little to compete with the moonlight, though the moon was not yet full. Tsurugu inhaled the cool air, scented with all the bursting new growth of spring, and felt muscles shift and twitch within him. "Shall we walk, Ookami-kun?"

They passed through the groomed courtyard into the artfully wild garden beyond. A number of gardeners spent uncounted hours cultivating the appearance of abandoned wilderness; it was an amusing thought to Tsurugu. He wished he'd thought to gather the legs of his *hakama* before coming out; the night dew drenched them so that they clung uncomfortably.

They had descended a little hill, skirting one of the artificial lakes, when Shishio held up a hand. "Is there someone here?" he asked softly.

Tsurugu stared into the night, listening. There was a faint sound, as of muffled movement, reflected by the still water. "I hear something, yes."

They moved about the shore of the lake toward a little stand of pines which divided garden areas. As they edged around the pines, they could see two light-colored figures moving together in the tall grass. Tsurugu's breath caught, and for a moment he thought of pale foxes.

But no, they were two human shapes. The twins were wrestling together in the field, stripped to the waist and careless in their play.

They leapt at one another, twisting first one and then the other to the ground before shoving apart and circling to begin anew. Their torsos were lean and muscular, perfect specimens of youth. They were laughing soundlessly, their mouths open in wide grins.

"How dare they use my lord's garden for their play?" Shishio drew his short sword, perhaps intending it for a disciplinary rod. *"Futago-me!"* he swore.

The twins broke apart and ran in opposite directions without even looking for the source of the shout. Shishio took a few steps forward and then hesitated, recognizing that he could not apprehend both and could not likely take either of them with such a start.

Tsurugu chuckled. "Did you expect them to stop and bow, waiting for you to arrive to beat them?"

"It is not as if they could not be identified," Shishio muttered, but his expression already was easing.

Tsurugu waved a hand in dismissal. "They are youths, and mere servants. We cannot expect good manners from them, and they have done no real harm."

"More, it is not my place to discipline them," Shishio agreed. "I am my lord's eye and hand, but not his staff. And they will likely be more careful in the future."

"I hope so."

Chapter 3

The moon-gazing party was not so large as some, but it was well-attended. Tsurugu was of no rank to sit with the great *daimyou* and other *samurai*, and so he found himself to one side of the garden, a little distance from the burbling stream which colored the conversation of the great ones.

The full moon hung bright over the garden, making it easy to see the broad ink strokes on the paper before him. He touched his brush again to the ink, considering. The guests were each writing poems on the beauty of the night, a chance to display good breeding and education to their peers, and while Tsurugu knew his poem would not be chosen as one of the most sensitive — he had an abhorrence for the overused metaphors of cherry blossoms and life's brevity — he wanted his poem to be complete in its own way.

One of the visiting *samurai* bent and placed a folded paper into the stream. It floated a little distance, until another plucked it from the water to add a few lines to the unfinished poem.

"Onmyouji-san, remain still," cautioned a voice.

Tsurugu carefully set his brush aside, adjusting his sleeve. "Good evening, Ookami-kun," he said without looking. "You have been watching for an imposter?"

"I have seen nothing suspicious," he confirmed. "These *samurai* are all known to me, if indirectly, and there is nothing to suggest they are not themselves."

Tsurugu glanced toward the wooden platform where, screened from male view, the women of the house also gazed and wrote poems. "Then she is safe another night."

"And my lord as well."

Naka no Yoritomo began to read a poem aloud, and Tsurugu resigned himself to leaving his own work unfinished. There would be other nights to gaze upon the moon. "I have been watching, myself," he confided. He stretched an arm toward the stream, and one of the folded poems lifted itself and, as if swept on a gentle breeze, came to his hand. "And I have found nothing to indicate that we should be concerned tonight — at least, not from *bakemono* or *mononoke*." He lifted a dish from his little writing table and sipped *sake*.

Time passed, and a prize poem was selected. Tsurugu did not pay attention to the awarding of a gift by the *daimyou*; he was thinking of the two youths playing carelessly in the lord's garden by moonlight.

A servant approached Naka no Yoritomo and bowed low. "Yoritomo-dono, my lady humbly asks that her servants be allowed to entertain this august assembly."

There was a moment of quiet shock — mere servants, entertain such *samurai*? But after a moment the *daimyou* nodded slowly. "If it is our lady's wish," he stated, "we will see her entertainers."

And who would argue? mused Tsurugu. The favored new wife of the powerful *daimyou*, in his own home — if the *daimyou* himself consented to it, none other could consider his own honor affronted.

One of Kaede's women moved behind the screen, and a place in the center of the garden cleared in anticipation of the coming performance. Guests murmured quietly. What would it be? Music? Reading?

It was the twins who moved smoothly and quietly into the open space, dressed in crisp light *hitatare*. Tsurugu sensed the growing interest of the party. They seemed to freeze mid-step as they reached the center, locked in position without even a rustle of robe to betray them, their eyes on the interlocked stones beneath their feet.

The musicians began to play, and the twins began to dance. It was not a dance like any of the court dances; this was something different, unknown. The two moved in unison, perfect synchronization, first in symmetry and then in complementary *kata*.

Guests leaned close, exchanging approving comments. It was not an art they knew, but they recognized its aesthetic quality, and they were pleased by it.

The twins moved fluidly, without any sense of effort, twisting and turning and gliding, limbs uncoiling sinuously as if they weighed nothing. Their faces remained impassive; their art was in movement, not expression. One produced a fan—from his corded sleeve, undoubtedly, though no one saw him reach for it—and then another, and then as they exchanged places four fans appeared to mark the tiniest shifts of hands and wrists.

Tsurugu brushed his thumb along his chin thoughtfully. The handsome twins would not want for company this night. Even now, poems of solicitation were being composed in the viewers' minds, he guessed, men and women alike. If the twins were wise, they would escape immediately upon completing their dance, ensuring they could claim ignorance of any unwanted invitation.

But they did not tire, and the liquid dance poured out of them for many minutes. It was impossible to guess if they followed the musicians or if the musicians followed them. And then finally, one of them turned and swept a *biwa* from its surprised master's hands, silencing the other players. As he turned back he plucked two final notes which hung quivering in the air, almost tangible in their flavor, as the dancers' movements slowed to imperceptibility and then, finally, stillness.

There was a rustle of movement, as the watching *samurai* seemed to draw themselves up from entrancement, and then as one the twins moved, returning the *biwa* and darting through the seated onlookers toward the house again, waiting for neither praise or comment.

"That is the same pair," came Shishio's low voice, "those dancers of such exquisite grace and manner, the same who were playing at rough-and-tumble in my lord's garden?"

"Remember," Tsurugu answered, "they are only servants. One should be more surprised that they showed such talent and beauty here than that they committed an offense before." Someone had risen to praise the performance; Tsurugu ignored him as he spoke to the hidden Shishio. "After all, they are not even entertainers, and it was only by the lord's permission that they were suffered to perform."

"They would have little trouble being adopted into a *samurai* family," Shishio answered, "and then they could serve as *ashigaru* in my lord's army. Or I myself would be glad of either — both! — in my own company."

Tsurugu smiled to himself, imagining the twins in soft grey, slipping unseen through the highest houses. "Perhaps. But I doubt Kaede-dono will allow them to leave her service so easily."

Chapter 4

Shishio and Tsurugu rode out the next day to examine the area about the shrine. "Here is where the wagon was left," Shishio pointed out, "and then they took this path."

Tsurugu looked up at the red *torii* marking the approach to the shrine. "They left their rice unattended?" he asked. "And then they complain it was stolen? This needs no *kitsune* mischief, Ookami-kun; this was no more than carelessness."

"I am inclined to agree with you," Shishio responded, looking up and down the hillside. "There is no visibility here at all, and while the victims claim to have been away for only a moment, one could hardly leave the wagon, reach the shrine, pray, and return so quickly. They must have been mistaken. Or, they are claiming the theft in order to withhold rice from my lord's tribute."

Tsurugu brushed his chin with his thumb, walking beneath the *torii*. "If there are bandits, you will find them out."

"With your help," Shishio added. "While this may have been human deed, there is still the matter of the *kitsune*, and I would be pleased to have your *onmyoudou* to counter any fox magic."

Tsurugu nodded. "I believe I will ride back now, Ookami-kun," he said. "I will see you this evening?"

"Yes, yes. I will look around for appropriate hiding places and then return."

Tsurugu was passing by rice fields when he heard the commotion. He reined about and saw the villagers shouting and shaking fists, occasionally striking something in their midst. At the edge of the group, a woman wailed and cried as others pushed her back.

So the unfortunate girl had not recovered; she was still in the hold of *kitsune-tsuki*, they believed, and may the Merciful Goddess protect her in what trial she would face now. Tsurugu frowned to himself. They were superstitious, these villagers, and it was known there was a *kitsune* nearby; nothing could save the girl from her fate.

He rode on another forty or fifty paces before he turned the horse back and urged it into a gallop.

The farmers quieted at his approach; they did not know him, of course, only that he was from the *daimyou*'s house. One came forward and bowed low. "How may we —"

"I am Tsurugu no Kiyomori, an *onmyouji* in the service of Naka no Yoritomo-dono," he interrupted. "I would like to examine and assist this — "

"Help her! Oh, good and kind lord, help her!" This must be the girl's mother, shrieking from the side as she bent to the dirt. "Save her!"

"Let me see her."

They brought her forward, holding her by the arms as she stared in shock rudely upward. One eye was swelling and she had bruises over her wrists, he noted; her hair was fallen and disheveled.

She would find no help here, he was certain. "Bind her," he ordered, "and give me the end of the rope. I will take her to a place where I may do what I can for her."

The mother wailed and fell to the ground, no doubt guessing at what might lie ahead for her helpless daughter. Tsurugu felt sorry for her — another time, she might have been correct. But he truly sought only to help the girl; his taste did not run to half-mad, bloodied females.

A farmer passed the end of a line to him, bowing and scraping, and Tsurugu wrapped it once about the saddle's pommel. The girl resisted briefly, but she could not hold back the horse, and at last she stumbled unhappily after him.

Tsurugu held the horse to a slow gait, though it was anxious to return to its stable, and then after a mile or so he turned off the road. There was a disused structure in this direction, he knew, perhaps known by the oldest residents here but certainly unvisited in many years. He had not come by the main road, and it had been in his interest to explore the area thoroughly before going to the *daimyou*'s house.

The building was several miles from the road. He reined the horse to a halt and turned in the saddle. "Come here, girl, and I will lift you onto the horse."

She stared at him, teary and afraid.

He silently cursed his conscience; his position was difficult enough without taking additional trouble. "There is no *kitsune* in you; trust me in this matter. You are your own. I wish to help you; you must trust me in that, too. Now come."

Slowly, hesitantly, she approached — for what would resisting avail her, in the end? — until he could reach down and take her upper arm, lifting her onto the protesting horse. She gripped the rear of the saddle with her bound hands, trying to avoid brushing him, and he nudged the horse forward again.

"I do not know whether your madness is real," he said, "or whether you have only offended some ignorant dog-loving farmer, but you may believe that there is no fox magic upon you."

She said nothing, and this did not concern him. She was only a village female, and one who had been called mad for some time. It had never been to her advantage to speak.

At last he stopped the horse and gestured for her to slide to the ground. She did, wide-eyed, and he dismounted. "I am going ahead," he told her, tying the rope to one tree and the horse's reins to another, "and then I shall return for you."

The hut was nearly where he'd remembered, beside a narrow stream of mountain snowmelt and well hidden within spring leaves. It had most likely been a hermit's refuge at one point, but it was long abandoned. It did not take him long to make his preparations, and then he led the silent, crying girl into the overgrown clearing, now almost reclaimed with young trees and spreading vines.

She dropped to her knees and began to weep, trembling. Tsurugu sighed and lifted her wrists, his narrow fingers probing the ropes. "Silly girl," he muttered. "I have told you that I only wish to help you." He withdrew his hands from the knots and interlaced his fingers. *"Kai!"*

The rope fell away, and she stared at him with fresh fear. "I am an *onmyouji*," he repeated patiently. "Now come inside."

The little shrine was battered and mossy on the outside, but as he led her through the fallen door, a new building seemed overlaid upon the old. A large fire burned merrily in one corner, before which a narrow bath steamed, and *tatami* covered the floor. Lanterns lit the room, flickering over a cooked meal. In one corner stood rolled sleeping mats beside folded robes, and in another stood a woman in servant's clothing, waiting with a welcoming smile.

The girl shrank back, clearly distrusting her eyes. "Don't be afraid," he said quickly. "I told you, I am an *onmyouji*. These are to help you. You fled once before, but you had to return; here you may stay for a time. This woman will assist you and help you to bathe, but then she will go outside and not return — do you understand? Then you may stay here for a time, until you have recovered yourself and chosen how to return to the village, or present yourself as a servant in the *daimyou*'s house, or go into the city for work."

She stared around her and then at him. "I — but I — when I said the traveling priest had — they said I...." Her voice faded, unable to finish.

"You are not mad," he said gently. "Take your peace here. What is your name, girl?"

She swallowed. "Murame."

"Murame-san, stay and rest. You will not see me again unless our paths decree it. Now, hurry; she will not last long after I go, and you will need her to help treat your wounds."

She dropped again to her knees. *"Doumo arigatou gozaimasu, onmyouji-sama!"*

He stepped backward and out the fallen door. He blinked and looked through the magic — a leaking building with one corner of its roof bending nearly to earth, dark but for the fire in the corner (the fire was real, if fueled by magic), a single dead rabbit to eat, and instead of mats and robes, only a strip torn from his own *haori*. But it would feel real to Murame, at least for a time. She had suffered enough for her reality; let her have some comfort within illusion.

He returned to his horse and started back to the *daimyou*'s house.

Chapter 5

Shishio placed a black stone on the game board, collected four white stones, and smiled at Tsurugu's discomfort. "Don't fret, my friend," he offered. "We can play the next as a teaching game if you like."

Tsurugu rolled his eyes. "Let us leave off playing altogether," he suggested. "I feel my time would be better spent elsewhere."

Shishio looked out the door at the softly falling rain. "It is not a night for walking in the garden or moon-gazing." He glanced back at Tsurugu with the air of someone about to broach a difficult question. "Perhaps you could show me the nature of your barriers about the house."

"If you like." Tsurugu turned and opened his writing box. "I can create a *kekkai* for you right here."

He selected a sheet of rice paper and began to grind ink. "Think of something from which you would like protection," he said. "Only, something very specific and very imminent, for the purpose of this demonstration. Ink, for example."

Shishio shrugged. "Ink, then."

"Very simple." Tsurugu drew out a five-pointed star. "Water, wood, fire, earth, metal. This is the basis of all." He smiled. "The rest is a bit more... esoteric."

He wrote a series of flowing *kanji* and then set aside the brush. His hands over the painted circle and characters, he closed his eyes and intoned soft syllables as his fingers worked through the *mudra*.

Shishio straightened on his knees. "The *kuji-in*?"

Tsurugu opened his eyes. "You are familiar with the nine syllables?"

Shishio looked vaguely uncomfortable. "I have heard of them." He gave a faint smile and grudgingly admitted, "Shadows work our own magic."

Tsurugu bit back his anxious questions; Shishio would not wish to explain. He reached for the writing brush, still wet with ink, and lay it over the back of his wrist. "Watch," he instructed, and he flicked the handle of the brush.

Ink shuddered from the brush and seemed to spread in the air over the rice paper, spattering over the surrounding *tatami*. The paper itself, protected by its invisible shield, showed not a drop of stray ink.

Shishio leaned forward eagerly. "Can this be used to defend against other substances? Steel, perhaps?"

"Not without some cost," Tsurugu warned. "A few drops of ink are simple to deflect; a blade driven with intent to kill is quite another. It is more efficient to use a like defense. But an evil *mononoke*'s attack is equally difficult to disrupt with a blade; it is more efficient to use a spirit defense."

"If like is used against like," Shishio said with a wry smile, "what would you do with the twins?"

"What, Genji and Kaworu?"

Shishio laughed aloud. "Surely those are more of your naming jests!"

Tsurugu chuckled. "I thought them appropriate. The twins are young and of low rank, but they are perhaps the most desired in the house. What better names than those of the greatest philanderers of literature?"

"Which is which?"

"Does it matter?"

"Well said. How would you protect yourself against them?"

"If I thought it necessary," Tsurugu began, taking a fresh sheet of rice paper, "I would gain control of them beforehand." He dipped his brush and wrote *Genji* and *Kaworu* in bold strokes. "And now I bind them." He slashed his finger horizontally above the paper. *"Rin."* The next movement was vertical. *"Byou."* He cut horizontally again, and then vertically. *"Tou, sha, kai, jin, retsu, zai, zen."*

Shishio nodded. "And now you have mastered them?"

"Or I would have, if those were their true names."

Shishio gestured toward the paper. "What of the *kitsune*?"

"Of course." Tsurugu inscribed *kitsune* on the paper and closed his eyes. *"Rin – byou – tou – sha – kai – jin – retsu – zai – zen!"*

"Well, onmyouji-san?"

"If we should meet the *kitsune* now," Tsurugu answered with a smile, "I will be the master of her."

Chapter 6

Shishio chose the night of the quarter moon to lay their trap for the rice thieves. Tsurugu dressed warmly — the late spring could still be chill on the mountainside — and went to the shrine early. Shishio would come singly and invisibly, and then the handful of warriors would take their places in hiding before the rice bait was left.

Tsurugu passed beneath the red *torii* and paused to kneel beside the white fox guardian statues. "Inari-sama," he breathed, "you bless all with rice and prosperity.... Protect your servants on this night, and guard us as we defend both rice and wealth." The prayer sounded cheeky, but he thought the goddess might like it; he had always privately assumed that any deity who chose mischievous foxes as messengers must have a sense of humor. "And, Inari-sama," he added more soberly, "bless the girl Murame, who has suffered at the hands of your rivals' servants and of her own people."

He rose, bowed once more, and then went to settle comfortably in his hiding place. He was not expected to fight as Shishio and the others would, though he would send *shikigami* to assist them.

The greatest *onmyouji* of old were alleged to command their *shikigami* as assassins, he mused. They must have had power he would never know.

Dusk fell, and the temperature with it. Tsurugu drew his knees to his chest, comfortable in the privacy of his hiding place, and wrapped his arms and voluminous sleeves about his legs. He rested his chin on his knees, warming his face in the fabric. He had been warned to keep still, lest they alert the thieves; he could wait comfortably like this for hours.

But they did not need to wait that long. There was a shout from below, nearer the road, and then a great rustling of leaves and feet as the warriors converged. A few voices cried in surprise and then pain. Tsurugu rose almost leisurely; it was no *kitsune*, as he had predicted. Shishio would need no protection from fox magic. Still, he ought to send a *shikigami* or two, to show support.

He reached for an overhanging branch and plucked a young leaf, holding it between his fingers as he breathed a spell. He released it and watched it float down toward the road, swirling in the night air. He sent another after it. Then, stretching his arms overhead, he started down the shrine path.

He felt the little burst of energy as the first leaf transformed. Surprised shouts informed him that his aim had been true; the apparent *mononoke* had appeared in the midst of the fighting. The second appeared immediately after, blocking retreat on the road. Tsurugu's smile vanished as he heard new screams, and he lifted his fingers, working a spell of discovery as he increased his pace down the path.

The *mononoke* had frightened the *daimyou*'s men as well as the all-too-human thieves, and all had scattered on the road. But he sensed others as well, near the combatants in the dark.

Tsurugu began to run through the night.

Chapter 7

Shishio cursed as he wielded his sword. His opponent fell, clutching his side, and Shishio finished him before running further into the woods.

The surprised thieves were neither supernatural *bakemono* nor common villagers, but a small pack of organized bandits, armed and trained to fight. The *daimyou*'s men had held the advantage of surprise until the *mononoke* had appeared in their midst, startling thief and warrior alike. They had each retreated into the woods and now were struggling to hide and seek, wanting to rejoin their comrades without alerting their opponents of their position.

It was a shadow wolf's dream, but the warriors were only *ashigaru* footmen, and he feared losing as many of them as he might take of the bandits.

It was utterly dark in the trees, the faint light of the quarter moon useless beneath the leaves. Shishio stood still, listening. He could hear men moving in several directions, but which were his own? Which were enemies?

Someone was hiding near him; he could hear suppressed breathing. He rotated slowly, feeling for secure footing and careful of branches impeding his coming strike. "For Naka no Yoritomo-dono!" he called sharply. "Speak!"

The hidden figure bolted with a sound of breaking vegetation.

Shishio's blow fell short, barely cutting the fast-moving target. There was a yelp in the darkness. He sprang forward to strike again.

Something rushed from the side and his blade met flesh. There was another cry, deeper this time, and then the sounds of flight. Shishio started to pursue, but footsteps led in two directions and quickly faded.

He paused and crouched low, keeping his sword ready. There would be others.

Chapter 8

The warriors gathered beside the rice wagon, examining their few wounds and grumbling angrily to one another. "Cursed sorcerer," snapped one. "When he comes, I'll cut him for—"

"How is that?" demanded Tsurugu, coming up the road. He clutched his left arm above the elbow. "I am here, and I am cut, but I will not concede that to you."

The warrior stood straighter before his watching companions. "You, onmyouji-dono, betrayed us with your *mononoke*!"

"Betrayed you?" repeated Tsurugu indignantly. "You were told, were you not, that I would send my servants among you to frighten the thieves? Were you, even warned, too timid to hold your ground as you were ordered?"

"Enough!" snapped the company's commander. "It is done; arguing will win nothing. And you dare not challenge an *onmyouji*," he added in a lower tone.

Tsurugu said nothing. He was exhausted, his arm hurt, and he owed nothing to these rude men.

"Form up," ordered the commander. He looked at Tsurugu. "Will you ride back with the rice?"

"No, I'll wait a bit," Tsurugu answered. "I want to examine the area and be sure that all negative energies have fled."

In truth, he was watching for Shishio, who emerged from the woods a quarter hour later. "Onmyouji-san! You are injured?"

"Not badly," Tsurugu told him. "Only a cut; it will heal. It was too dark in the woods to tell friend from foe."

"Indeed. There were moments when I could not tell what I struck, only that he had not spoken the counter-phrase."

"You will return now?"

"Not just yet. I think I owe the goddess thanks for her benevolence this night."

He bound Tsurugu's arm for later attention and they started up the steep path. It was not long before they passed the first of the red *torii*. "I would like to make an offering," Shishio said. "Perhaps I'll return with one. We might have fared much worse. But, onmyouji-san! your *mononoke* frightened even me! Great slavering fangs of a *bakeneko* — you might have warned me!"

"What has the appearance of a *bakeneko* to do with a shadow wolf?" teased Tsurugu.

He glanced ahead to the shrine and faltered. "What—"

They ran together for the figure slumped upon the step. Shishio reached him first and seized the young man's shoulder, rolling him back to show his face—one of the twins.

Tsurugu placed a hand over his face, concentrating. "He is injured, but not seriously. He will recover."

"He is not wounded," said Shishio wonderingly. "There's no mark on him. Was it spiritual energy?"

Tsurugu nodded distractedly.

"But how did he come here?"

The young man seemed to wake, drawing back from Shishio's hold and looking anxiously from Shishio to Tsurugu.

"Why are you here?" demanded Shishio. "Were you with the bandits?"

The young man's eyes widened.

"Did you fight with them?"

He shook his head, looking between them.

Shishio cuffed him. "Don't you speak?"

He shook his head again, shrinking back.

"Did you follow the soldiers?" intervened Tsurugu. "You thought there would be excitement to watch?"

The servant dropped his eyes and nodded.

Tsurugu sighed and sat back. "There you have it. Your brother, too?"

He nodded again, but with fresh worry; it seemed he did not know where his brother was.

Shishio frowned. "But how could he come to arcane injury so near the shrine, and when your terrifying *mononoke* was only a *shikigami*?"

"Clearly there are other forces at work." Tsurugu thumbed at his chin.

"The *kitsune*?"

"I—I don't know." He looked at the single twin. "Go and find your brother, and return to the house."

The servant nodded eagerly and scrabbled backward before bowing low on the ground. Then he turned and ran from the shrine without looking back.

"Strange, they are," commented Shishio. "Twins, and without speech. They might be *bakemono* themselves." He frowned. "Do you think they could be *kitsune*, onmyouji-san?"

Tsurugu was already kneeling before the shrine, addressing thanks to Inari.

"Onmyouji-san?"

"I will think on it," answered Tsurugu shortly, "and we may speak of it later."

On their way back to the *daimyou*'s house, Tsurugu saw across a rice field two figures rush together, throwing themselves about one another and then dipping and wheeling in playful celebration. He did not point out the reunion to Shishio.

Chapter 9

There was a training exercise for the *ashigaru* the next day, and Shishio went to a high tower to watch. On the grassy field below servants struggled with dogs of various sizes while the *samurai* mounted their excited horses. Around Shishio others gathered to look down; an *inuoumono*, a dog hunt, would be full of action.

On some signal the dogs were released. Some began to run across the field, as if they knew what awaited; others bounded to entice their fellows to play or circled an attractive female. And then the *samurai* came, pushing their galloping horses directly at the dogs, who scattered before the hooves in sudden panic. The warriors drew their man-height bows and targeted dog after dog. Shishio could hear the frightened and pained yelps from his lofty vantage point.

A small movement to his left drew his attention, and he saw one of the twins staring fixedly at the field. He could not tell if it were the same one they'd found at the shrine. The servant clenched his fists and seemed to twitch with each release of the bow.

Was he disturbed by the hunt? There were a few who did not like the slaughter, though the dogs were given the sporting chance to run and it provided excellent training on moving targets for the archers. Perhaps this talented dancer was too sensitive for military exercise. "Don't you like it?" Shishio asked.

The young man hardly glanced at Shishio, his shoulders jerking with some emotion. "*Inu ga kirai,*" he breathed, so that Shishio could hardly hear. *I hate dogs.*

Shishio stared at him a moment. So they could speak! or one, at least.

The servant seemed to come to himself, looking suddenly at Shishio with wide eyes. He bowed hastily and then ran, disappearing into the house before Shishio could think to question him.

Chapter 10

Shishio threw open Tsurugu's door without ceremony. "Onmyouji-san! Come immediately!"

Tsurugu was halfway to his feet. "What is it?"

"I have been a fool! It is Kaede-dono herself!"

Tsurugu stared at him. "What?"

"Come with me!" As they hurried around the house, Shishio explained. "I was in the yard and I happened to turn back toward my lady's rooms. The light was just right to throw their silhouettes upon the *shouji* — and I saw the shadow of a fox. Kaede-dono is the *kitsune* herself!"

Tsurugu's mind raced. "Have you told the *daimyou*?"

"Not yet. He is quite taken with her; we must capture her and reveal her true form before we go to him."

They had arrived at the lady's rooms. Shishio addressed the woman at the door. "The *onmyouji* Tsurugu no Kiyomori and the *daimyou*'s servant have come to speak with my lady on a matter of gravest importance."

There was a brief flurry of activity to settle the lady safely behind a screen before they could enter. Shishio and Tsurugu lowered themselves to the floor and bowed low. "Kaede-dono," Shishio began, "my lord has entrusted Tsurugu-san and myself with the finding of the *kitsune* which plagues this area."

"I know this, Shishio Hitoshi-san," answered Kaede from behind the screen. She had a lovely voice; it was easy to recognize why Naka no Yoritomo loved her. "Yoritomo-dono has told me all this."

Shishio hesitated, clearly surprised that she knew him. "Then, Kaede-dono," he recovered, glancing nervously at Tsurugu, "you will understand our caution and our thoroughness."

Tsurugu nodded, drawing the *kanji* for *kitsune* in the palm of his left hand. With his right he began to trace the grid that would bind the creature to his will.

Heartened, Shishio continued, "Then, Kaede-dono, you will explain why your silhouette upon the *shouji* was that of a fox."

Kaede laughed, the silky, cultured sound of a well-bred and wealthy woman. "My silhouette? Shishio-san, you have made a mistake."

"My lady —"

"No, let me set your mind at ease. Hanae-san?"

A maid moved smoothly across the room, bearing a lantern to the lady. Tsurugu watched as the maid passed behind the screen and set the lamp carefully behind her mistress.

"Is that enough, or do you require more light?"

The shadow flickering between them was certainly that of a woman, and nothing else. Tsurugu's heart caught in his chest as she chuckled in her rich voice.

Shishio threw himself to the floor. "Great lady, I beg your forgiveness...."

Tsurugu bowed low as well. Such a mistake might mean death.

"Do not fear, honorable servants," Kaede assured them. "I am not affronted. You must have seen a trick of the light, but your intentions to protect my lord were true." She paused. "But you might have known sooner, Shishio Hitoshi-san, as I have greeted you by name, and it is common knowledge that a fox cannot say *shi*." She sounded amused at his lapse.

"I crave your pardon, Kaede-dono."

"Tsurugu-san?"

Tsurugu's stomach clenched within him. "How may I serve you, Kaede-dono?"

"I am told you rendered some assistance to one of my servants."

"One of the twins, yes, though I did very little."

The smile was evident in her voice. "They have names."

"Genji and —" Tsurugu caught himself.

"What? What do you call them?"

Tsurugu gave the shocked Shishio an agonized glance. "Genji and Kaworu, my lady."

She laughed again, longer than before. "You read a woman's tales, Tsurugu-san. But I thank you for your service to me in protecting my servant."

"It was my pleasure and honor to serve you, Kaede-dono."

They bowed their chagrined way from the lady's quarters and fled to Tsurugu's room. "Merciful Goddess," moaned Shishio, "we could have—I might have—merciful Kannon, how could I have made such a mistake?"

"And involved me?" Tsurugu added fiercely. "I had not even seen the shadow, and your precipitate action would have killed me as well!"

Shishio bowed to him. "I beg your forgiveness. This *kitsune* is driving me to madness without even her touch."

"And me as well," Tsurugu relented. "Or I should not have mocked the servants Kaede-dono obviously favors."

"We must find this fox," Shishio said firmly. "You must set your *shikigami* to tracking her, you must lay *kekkai* to confound her. We must find her."

There was the softest of sounds at the door, as if a demure lady begged to enter, but it was the twins who came into the room. They set aside two small tables and bowed low, their posture precisely correct. Tsurugu wondered if their scare on the mountain had made them more mannerly. Then they presented the tables and backed away.

Upon each table rested a lacquered box. Shishio glanced nervously at Tsurugu. A gift? Poison? What could follow so hard upon such an insult?

But within each box lay only a slip of colored paper, violet for Shishio and a soft russet for Tsurugu.

"A shadow upon *shouji*

becomes something to

cherish

for the laugh it brings.

This self is complimented

with the grace of *kitsune*.

As these excellent

servants have proven amusing to

you, I hope they will prove as

useful. If Genji and Kaworu can

assist you in your task, do not

hesitate to utilize them.

Shishio gave Tsurugu a long-suffering
look.

Tsurugu looked at the two young men
waiting motionless before them. *"Dochira ga
Kaworu deshou ka?" Which is Kaworu, I wonder?*

One of them bobbed slightly in his bow.

"Then I will want you to carry an offering to the shrine of Inari."

The servant bowed lower again in acknowledgment.

Chapter 11

Tsurugu left his horse and picked his way through the trees to the abandoned hermitage. "Hello?" he called.

"Onmyouji-sama!" Murame knelt in the doorway.

He looked around the decrepit building; the magic had faded only a little. "How are you faring?"

"Very well, onmyouji-sama. The maid left, as you said she would, but I am accustomed to caring for myself.... I worried for food, but I am finding what I need in the forest. I need very little."

You will need more soon enough, thought Tsurugu. In another span of days, her sleeping mats would be merely a strip of torn *haori* again. "Have you thought of where you will go?"

"Oh, yes, onmyouji-sama. I will present myself as a maidservant to the house of the *daimyou*. I know they sought servants during the winter; the lord's new wife makes more hands necessary."

Tsurugu smiled to himself. "You should go soon," he said. "The magic here will not last much longer."

Still, the illusion had remained intact longer than he had anticipated. He stepped past her into the makeshift house and looked around. All was nearly as he had left it. He looked at the table where she had been preparing a meal (a small mouse, though she would see it as a pheasant) and saw a ball about the size of a woman's fist, white and iridescent. "Where did you find that?"

"I found it in the forest, onmyouji-sama. I thought it was pretty. Have I done wrong?"

"No, not wrong," he answered slowly, "but you would do well to let me take it." He picked up the ball and balanced it on his palm, where it seemed to glisten.

This was a *hoshi no tama*, a star-stone, the prized possession of nearly all *kitsune*. A fox must be careless or frightened to lose its magic ball. "When did you find it?"

"A few days ago, my lord. The day following the fighting at the shrine."

Of course, the shrine would be an easy walk from the hermitage. Perhaps an observing *kitsune* had lost its *hoshi no tama* in the fright of the fighting.

The magic of the ball had kept the illusion strong. Now, however, Murame needed the magic to dissipate, so that she would go to the *daimyou*, and he needed the ball. It was incontrovertible proof that a *kitsune* had come near. He tucked it securely into his clothing.

Chapter 12

Tsurugu sat in his room, reading over an *onmyoudou* text and sipping occasionally at *sake*. It was late in the night when Shishio entered. "Forgive my intrusion, onmyouji-san, but I saw your light and I have news which cannot wait."

"Sit and tell me," Tsurugu invited.

Shishio brought out a folded sheet. "One of my men has finally sent me word," he explained. "I had sent him to ask questions of the Fujitani, about Kaede-dono."

Tsurugu's pulse quickened. "Ookami-kun...."

Shishio ignored his warning tone. "It is not the lady herself. In fact, she is not herself at all—she is not Fujitani no Kaede but Yamakawa no Kaede! She lied about being one of the Fujitani because, onmyouji-san, the Yamakawa are *kitsune-mochi*. Fox-possessors."

Tsurugu began to sweat beneath his *oukatabira*. "*Kitsune-mochi?*"

"They bind *kitsune* as their servants. You see it now? It is not Kaede-dono who is the *kitsune*; that is why she could display her shadow and pronounce my name. It is a servant—perhaps more than one. The twins, almost certainly."

Tsurugu held up a hand, trying to think. "They would not have been in her room where you saw the shadow—"

"Then that was another fox, perhaps the maid. She could have remained safely behind the lamp which proved her mistress innocent. We must go and—"

"No!" burst Tsurugu. "You cannot accuse her again! Not without—"

"We will have proof," Shishio assured him. "Let us go secretly to her rooms and observe—"

Tsurugu stared at him in open shock. "Observe the lady!"

"—And we will dispel the fox magic with our own, so that we may see if she has *kitsune* with her or not. Come, hurry!"

Tsurugu made to protest again, but Shishio was already going out, and so he leapt to his feet to follow.

Shishio knew the ways of the *daimyou*'s house, and he led Tsurugu to a place in the garden where they could stealthily ease a *shouji* to the side and peer into the lady's rooms. Tsurugu shifted uneasily, liking none of this, but he did not know how to stop his friend. He could not accuse the lady Kaede without proof; he would not be dissuaded.

Flowering bushes shielded them from anyone walking late in the garden, and there were no lanterns near their hiding place. They might not be seen, after all.

From their place, they could watch the maid Hanae comb Kaede's glossy hair which puddled on the floor behind her; it would reach to her ankles when she stood. Beyond the screen, two figures approached and bowed low. "Kaede-dono," one began quietly, "we have been careless."

"She receives male servants?!" gasped Shishio.

"It is lost," said the other figure, "one of our *tama*. We lost it on the mountain."

Tsurugu thought of the retrieved *hoshi no tama* safe within his robes.

"Let us dispel this fox magic now," urged Shishio. "Come...." He closed his eyes

and clasped his fingers in the first of the
mudra. "*Rin!*"

"Wait," whispered Tsurugu.

"*Byou!*"

Energy began to move about them,
shifting the air without breeze.

"*Tou!*"

Tsurugu felt the magic swelling like a
wave. Hair began to prickle at the base of his
neck.

"*Sha!*"

Hanae's shadow shifted beyond the
lantern, showing a more elongated skull.

"*Kai!*"

The prickling ran over all of Tsurugu's
body now as the fox magic ebbed. He
shuddered.

"*Jin!*"

Hanae gasped as she saw red fur
appear upon her hands.

"Retsu!"

The twins shifted in the lantern light, becoming adolescent foxes with pale fur, bowing before Kaede.

"Zai!"

Kaede sat upright, alarm on her face, and she looked about the room. She snapped an order to the servants.

"Zen!" Shishio reached for Tsurugu's arm. "Three! She has three, at the least! We shall tell Yoritomo-dono and-"

His hand closed on fur and he whirled to stare at Tsurugu. The fox snapped at his wrist as Shishio reached for a weapon and it leapt at him. Shishio fell backward as nails scraped his face.

His hand found the fox and dragged it away from his eyes. Teeth sank into his thumb as he drew his *wakizashi* to strike. The fox writhed in his grip.

Hands grasped him and forced him to the earth, pinning his head and arms. Shishio could not twist free. The fox squirmed and grew too large to hold, and then Tsurugu was kneeling upon his chest.

"You shall tell no one, Ookami-kun," Tsurugu growled through unnaturally pointed teeth. On either side, Genji and Kaworu held fistfuls of Shishio's hair and crouched upon his wrists.

"*Kitsune-me!*" Shishio swore. "You will —"

"Listen to me," Tsurugu intoned fiercely, fully human once more. "My lady loves Yoritomo-dono, and we have done him no harm."

"You are *kitsune* within his house!"

"And we have done well for our lords! Your master as well — we have brought him greater wealth while Kaede-dono was courted and wed."

"Tainted gifts! *Kitsune* are not to be trusted!"

"Would you betray your lord's trust by destroying his honor? By shaming his love?"

"I would see you dead and my lord's house purged of your foul magic!"

"Hear me, Ookami-kun; I would not —"

Shishio wrenched beneath the twins and heaved himself upward. One arm broke free and he reached for Tsurugu.

Tsurugu drove his flattened fist into Shishio's charge, snapping the man's head backward. He snatched the *wakizashi* from Shishio's numbed fingers and drew the short blade across his throat.

Blood sprayed across the three *kitsune*. Shishio tried to cry out as he wrenched beneath their hold, but there was only a soft burbling as he bled.

"I am sorry, Ookami-kun." Tsurugu regarded him sadly. "You shall not interfere with our mistress." He looked at the twins, their *kimono* already spotless within the illusionary fox magic. "Bury him well," he instructed softly. "He was honorable to his charge."

Thanks for reading Kitsune-Tsuki*! Did you enjoy it? Please leave an honest review — I read every one, and I'd really appreciate it!*

Read on for a sample from **Kitsune-Mochi**, the next in the series! Want to know more about the world of *Kitsune Tales*? Read about the folklore behind the stories at **www.LauraVanArendonkBaugh.com**. Sign up for news, sneak peeks, and a free story. Your email will never be shared.

About the Author

Laura VanArendonk Baugh CPDT-KA KPACTP was born at an early age and never looked back. She works in animal behavior by day and haunts Japanese culture and anime/manga conventions by night. Find her and get a free story at:

www.LauraVanArendonkBaugh.com.

Kitsune-Mochi

The *onmyouji* Tsurugu no Kiyomori and his allies must protect his *daimyou*'s household from a dangerous rival without revealing their own secret—or they die by the hands of their friends instead of their enemies.

Chapter One

"Kagemura no Shishio Hitoshi would never have deserted his duty. If he cannot be found, he must be dead." Naka no Yoritomo fixed unyielding eyes on Tsurugu. "How has this happened?"

Tsurugu bowed low. "I am sorry, *tono*. I cannot say."

Naka no Yoritomo's voice darkened. "I have paid well for an *onmyouji* so I would know exactly the dangers we face. I brought you to learn if a *kitsune* were present, and I set Shishio Hitoshi to assist you. Is this how my generosity is rewarded?"

Tsurugu Kiyomori had not come for the gold, but that was not for Naka-dono to hear. "*Onmyoudou* gives many insights and a great deal of power, *tono*. It does not make us like the gods themselves."

The *daimyou's* voice quieted. "Tsurugu-sama, I have lost my eye, my hand, my shadow." Tsurugu's gut tightened. "What happened to him?"

"I cannot say."

"You cannot say? Or you do not know?"

Tsurugu swore silently.

"Tsurugu-sama, I do not know even whether Shishio-san was lost to a *bakemono* or to a rival house, whether the danger is political or supernatural. I must have information, if I am to protect my house, my people, my bride."

"Be patient a short time, *tono*, and I will try to have an answer. With your permission, I will come again in one hour."

He retreated to his room and seated himself before the *chokuban*, the divining board marked with stars and directions and lunar mansions. He would need no *onmyoudou* to answer the *daimyou*'s question, but it would be good to make an appropriate show for the servants.

He worked the desultory divination, his hands knowing the motions on the *chokuban* while his thoughts wandered. He had liked and respected Shishio Hitoshi, had even been his friend in an odd way, and he had never wished him harm. Even at the end, if there had been any way to speak reasonably to him, if Shishio had not tried to attack once more —

His fingers stuck on the *chokuban*, and Tsurugu looked down, startled. He blinked and reset the device, turning the stars to align with the myriad other markings, but the result was the same.

Was it *karma*, already?

He was still staring at the divination results when a sound at the door caught his attention. It was one of the *daimyou*'s pages, trying to look self-important while peeking at the divination materials. Tsurugu held up a hand to forestall the prompt. "I'm ready."

When he returned, Fujitani no Kaede was seated near her husband, screened from Tsurugu's view with only a bit of multi-layered train artfully displayed. He knelt, bowed, and then straightened to answer them. "*Oyakata-sama, okugata-sama*, I have something to report of your lost servant."

"Please, speak."

Tsurugu bowed again, an excuse to hide his face. "He died at the hands of the *kitsune* you feared. He discovered it and fought it and was killed."

Yoritomo was surprised. "But—*kitsune* do not often kill."

"No, they do not." Tsurugu could hear unsteadiness in his voice. "But he had trapped this one, and it seems it had no other chance to escape. It killed him and bore away his corpse. I am very sorry."

"Rise, Tsurugu-sama, there is no need for apology in this. It was not your doing that Shishio fell in his duty." The *daimyou* frowned. "Though it is unlike him to have acted alone, without informing me—or asking you to join him, when you were brought specifically to counter the *kitsune*."

"He may have come upon the creature while it was trapped or weakened, *tono*, perhaps changing forms or otherwise hampered," came Kaede's rich voice. "He might have thought the opportunity too rare to lose."

Tsurugu nodded. "If the creature had no other escape...." Though humans killed the trickster spirits, *kitsune* did not often kill humans. It was almost unthinkable. Nearly unbearable.

Naka no Yoritomo sighed. "Still, a mistake, and one which has cost us all. Tsurugu-sama, do you wish to add something?"

Tsurugu clenched his fists, fearing what the *daimyou* had seen in his face. "No, *tono*. It is only — he was my friend."

Naka no Yoritomo nodded. "We will honor him."

Dismissed, Tsurugu fled to his room, where he hugged his knees close and pressed his face into them. If Shishio had not been stopped, they would all have suffered, even died — Tsurugu, the twins, Hanae, and Fujitani no Kaede herself. He had done what was necessary. He could not allow harm to come to Kaede-dono, and it was foolish not to protect his own life. What had been done was now done.

And he had new matters to occupy him.

He waited until evening, when fireflies came out to play among the yard's carefully arranged stones. Tsurugu rose, bound his *hakama* to his legs so the fabric would not sag damply with dew, and went out into the night. They would meet in the far reaches of the garden, in the artful wilderness beyond the house. There were few secrets within a house of moving walls.

The twins were there already, rolling in the grass in their play. One glanced up as Tsurugu approached, and his brother promptly pinned him. "Unfair!" yelped the one in the wet grass.

"*Konbanwa*, Kiyomori-sama," greeted the upper youth. He slid from his position of advantage and leaned lazily upon his reclining brother.

They had, in private moments, little appreciation for the delicacies of rank, though at least Tsurugu had been accorded his proper honorific. "Up, you two," Tsurugu admonished mildly. "You're soaking."

The twins rolled up from the flattened grass with wide grins. Genji and Kaworu — Tsurugu had facetiously named them for the irresistibly handsome philanderers of the popular novel — were identical to the casual human eye. They were Fujitani no Kaede's servants, brought to the household when she married Naka no Yoritomo. They were excellent dancers as well, despite their lowly status in the household, and almost never seen singly.

"While we are alone...." Tsurugu withdrew from his clothes a plum-sized ball, iridescent in the moonlight. He let the *hoshi no tama* roll over his fingers, toying with it. "Which of you lost this?"

Genji held out a hand. "It is mine, Ki-san."

"See that you do not lose it again. And do not call me Ki-san."

"Ki-sama, then."

Tsurugu cuffed him. "There are limits, Genji-kun."

Genji made a face. "My *tama*?"

"Tsurugu Kiyomori-san," called a lilting voice, "please finish your business, so we may join you without recalling that one of these had carelessly lost something precious."

Genji retreated a few steps, tucking the ball safely within his clothing. He and Kaworu bowed as Kaede-dono, followed closely by her maid Hanae, came to join them.

Tsurugu bowed as well. "*Konbanwa*, Kaede-dono." He straightened. "And the *tama* was not found by anyone who knew its nature. There was no danger of it betraying us."

"Only through good fortune." Kaede looked at the twins, rumpled and damp. "*Ara*, what a disheveled mess you look. This will never do when—"

"*Okugata-sama!*" A voice rang through the garden, and a torch flared beyond a line of trees. "Kaede-dono! *Okugata-sama!*"

"I am here alone," Kaede ordered in a hushed tone.

Tsurugu nodded, and there was a brief blur of colors as his vision shifted. A moment later, he was a fox, disappearing into the hydrangeas and flattening himself to the ground. A few paces away, two pale young foxes slipped into the darkness.

Hanae draped a robe across the ground; safe with her mistress, she had no reason to hide. Kaede sank upon the robe. "Here I am," she called. "Who's there?"

There was a crash of foliage as someone came nearer, raising the torch. "Kaede-dono! We have—"

"Stay where you are!" snapped Hanae with uncharacteristic authority. "Your lady is unveiled."

Kaede raised a silk sleeve to conceal herself from the torchlight, as ladies of rank were not to be viewed by servants or strangers. "I came out to gaze upon the moon, and to think upon a poem. Has my lord called for me?"

"I beg your pardon, Kaede-dono. You were missed, and there was an alarm.... The *kitsune*...."

Kaede rolled her eyes behind her sleeve. "The *onmyouji* has given me a charm which he promised would protect me for this evening. I thank you for your concern, but I am perfectly safe."

"We could not find the *onmyouji* when we went for him."

Even behind her sleeve, Kaede had the presence of mind to resist glancing at the flowering bush hiding Tsurugu's fox form. Kaede always had great presence of mind. "It is possible he went out as well, for it is a lovely night. You may find him yet, and soon if you keep up this racket. Tell my lord Yoritomo-dono that I am found, that I am safe, and that I beg him to join me in my room shortly."

"Yes, my lady." The torch moved away.

Kaede lowered her sleeve; her *kitsune* had the intimate privilege of looking upon her. "Come, we must finish quickly."

Three foxes slid from hiding places and faced her, becoming human once more. The twins were grinning; Tsurugu would have to warn them against teasing the searching servants before returning to the house.

"Very briefly," Kaede said, "Midorikawa-dono is coming."

Tsurugu heard an intake of breath, almost too soft to note, and when he looked, the twins' grins had vanished. "When?" he asked.

"In a fortnight or so. I will tell you when he's come."

As if they would need telling.... The arrival of Midorikawa-dono would stir every *youkai* in the mountain. And with the warnings he had seen.... Tsurugu would be kept busy, for the *daimyou*'s household would surely notice the increased supernatural activity.

"Now go, and leave no suspicion." Kaede gestured.

Tsurugu bowed. Beside him, the twins became pale foxes once more and slipped into the darkness. He did not worry that they would find trouble. The news of Midorikawa-dono would have quelled their taste for excitement.

Follow the adventures of Kaede-dono and her *kitsune* companions, along with a host of *oni*, *tengu*, *kappa*, and others in *Kitsune-Mochi*.